# SHELBO'S
## Adventures in
# SCIENCE
## Natural Light and Man-made Light

# Michelle L. Dean

Tellwell Talent
www.tellwell.ca

ISBN
978-0-2288-4485-3 (Paperback)

# Acknowledgments

To my precious family Michael, McCormick, McKeon, and McQuade I love you very much. Thank you for all your support. A special thank you to Angelia, Jodie, and Karen for always being there for me. You are the "Originals." To my Mom and Dad, I love you forever and a day. To my United Way family thank you for believing in me. A huge shout out to John and Sonya for all your prayers.

There are two different kinds of light. Shelbo will explain with such delight. One is called natural and the other is man-made. These types of lights will never fade.

Natural lights are made with God's hands from up above. He made them with a heart filled with love.

These lights are tried and true without them Shelbo wouldn't know what to do. Some are big and some are small. Let's count them, count them, count them all.

It shines so bright and lights our way. It warms our skin on a hot summer's day. Can you guess what it may be? It's the sun that helps us see!

1 sun

The stars, the stars, twinkle and shine. Their light is of the most beautiful kind. At a quick glance, they twinkle and dance. Lights at night can be so bright. Shelbo makes a wish this very night.

**2 stars**

Fire is a natural light too. It crackles and pops and can sometimes look blue.

**3 blue fires**

During a storm, there can be lightening. Sometimes it can be quite frightening. The clouds roll in while the thunder begins to rumble. While holding your umbrella in the rain be careful not to stumble.

**4 lightning strikes**

I see a light...I'm not sure why. Fireflies dancing in the darkened sky. On and off they flicker and dance. Do you think Shelbo can catch one by chance?

**5 fireflies**

Some special jellyfish have lights inside. They move through the water glowing with pride. In the ocean, they squeeze their bodies forward. Sometimes they turn shoreward.

6 jellyfish

Man-made lights are made by man. Thomas Edison had a plan. He created a light bulb it's plain to see. After he did, he shouted with glee.

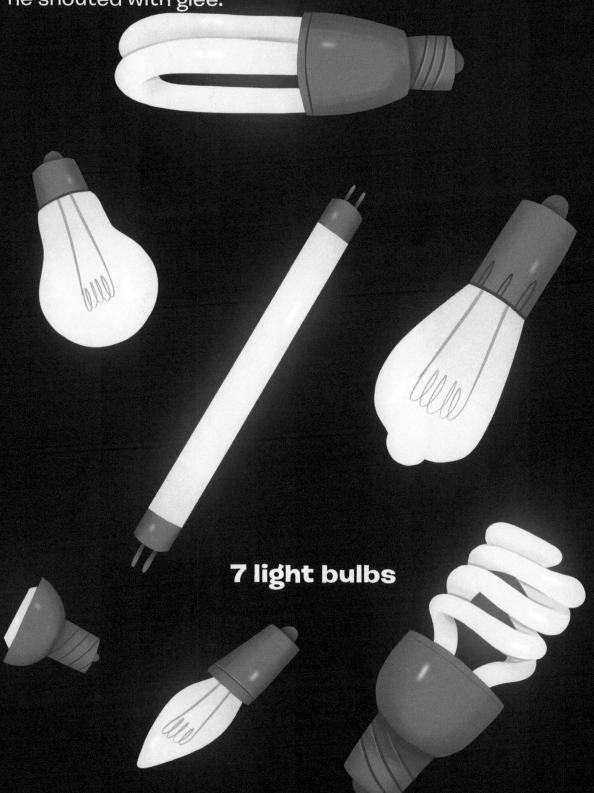

**7 light bulbs**

Flashlights help us see in the dark. Even if we are at the park. Big ones, small ones, short ones, tall ones. When walking in the dark at night, we need their marvelous light.

**8 flashlights**

Lamps are made to help us see. Inside our house not in a tree. We turn them off and then on. Until we begin to yawn.

**9 lamps**

**10 neon lights**

Televisions are a type of man-made light. They can fill your heart with such delight. I see a commercial showing a toy. I want that, I want that, oh boy... oh boy! It has a light at the top. Come on keep reading and do not stop!

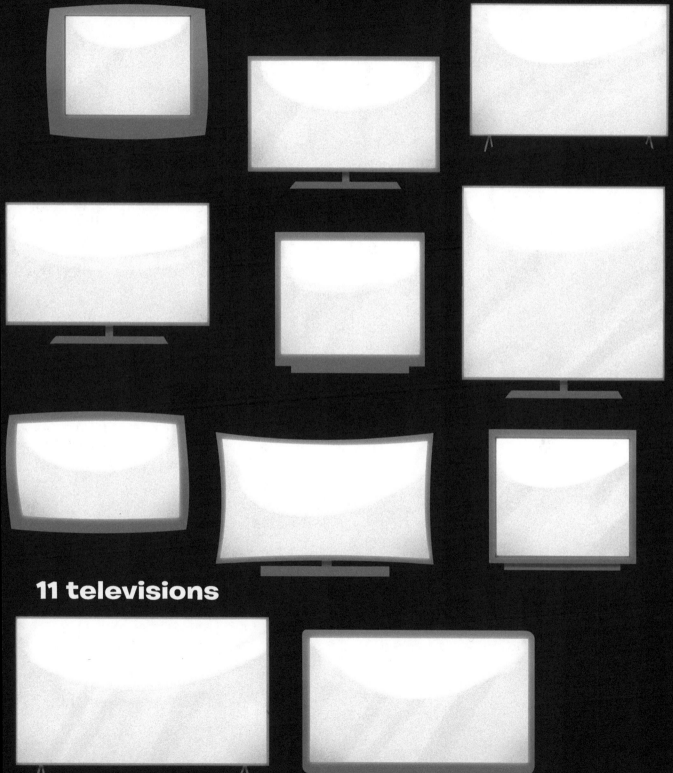

**11 televisions**

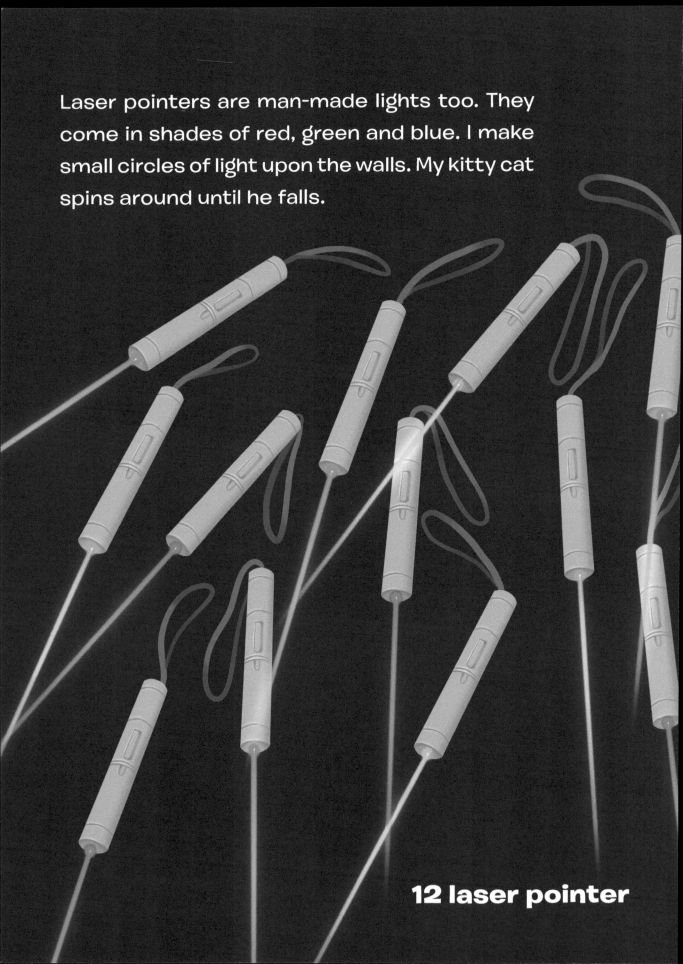

Laser pointers are man-made lights too. They come in shades of red, green and blue. I make small circles of light upon the walls. My kitty cat spins around until he falls.

**12 laser pointer**

Lights are important for you and me. In many ways, they can help us see. Scientists have done their part. They really are very smart.

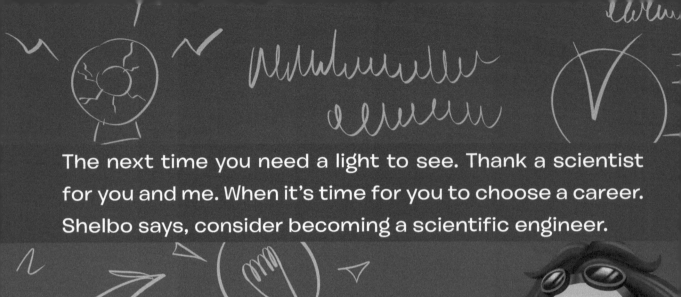

The next time you need a light to see. Thank a scientist for you and me. When it's time for you to choose a career. Shelbo says, consider becoming a scientific engineer.

You can make a difference Shelbo has no doubt. It really makes her want to shout. Hurry, Hurry you must not delay! God will help you come what may.

Think of ways to light your path. You will need to use some simple math. Look to the future and make things new. You can be an inventor that is truer than true.

Look in the mirror and take a stand.
Tell yourself I can...I can!

Open your eyes and open the door. Create your ideas and say once more: I can do it...it's plain to see. I am amazing as can be. I have a future as a scientist. I truly am a finalist!

Science, science is for me! I am as happy as can be. I can invent amazing light machines because I have scientific dreams!

Now we've come to the end, I hope you will be Shelbo's new friend. Shelbo has more adventures to share with you. Until next time too-da-loo.

CPSIA information can be obtained
at www.ICGtesting.com
Printed in the USA
LVHW072300150421
684696LV00004B/14